Kula and the Old 'Ukulele

written by Lance Wheeler
illustrated by Jon J. Murakami

Mutual Publishing

Copyright © 2007 by Mutual Publishing, LLC

All rights reserved. No part of this book may be reproduced in any form or by any electronic or mechanical means, including information storage and retrieval devices or systems, without prior written permission from the publisher, except that brief passages may be quoted for reviews.

Library of Congress Cataloging Data available upon request.

ISBN-10: 1-56647-844-8
ISBN-13: 978-1-56647-844-1

First Printing, October 2007

Mutual Publishing, LLC
1215 Center Street, Suite 210
Honolulu, Hawai'i 96816
Ph: 808-732-1709 / Fax: 808-734-4094
email: info@mutualpublishing.com
www.mutualpublishing.com

Printed in Taiwan

I would like to dedicate this book to
my wife and muse, Kimberly,
and my precious son, Kula.
They light my world.
—L.W.

Kula's old Tūtū Kāne had almost no money.
He had barely enough to eat.
His lauhala hat was all shredded up,
and his T-shirt was torn at the sleeves.

His baggy blue jeans were no longer blue;
they were faded and patched at the knees.
And if not for a pair of old rubber slippers,
he wouldn't have shoes on his feet.

So on his eighth birthday, Kula told Tūtū Kāne,
"For my birthday, I don't want a thing.
I don't want more than I already have,
and what I don't have I don't really need."

Tūtū Kāne was moved,
and he barely could speak.
His eyes welled like tide pools,
and tears wet his cheeks.

"You are so special," Tūtū Kāne replied.
Kula hugged his old Tūtū as he wiped his eyes.
"But I do have a gift for you this special day.
It'll fill you with hope no matter what comes your way."

So from next to his bed among ipu and mele,
Tūtū Kāne gave Kula an old 'ukulele.

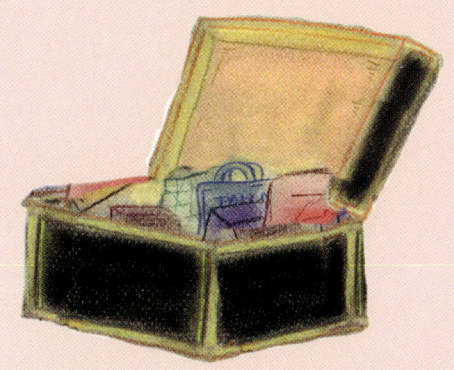

Kula's eyes filled with wonder. He plucked out each note, fingers dancing like fleas, as Tūtū Kāne had hoped.

"You're a natural, little Kula. An 'ukulele star! If you keep practicing, you'll really go far."

Kula practiced all night,
and all through the week.
He only stopped playing
to shower and eat.

He plucked and he strummed
and he practiced all day.
He wrote his own songs
and danced as he played.

Then early one morning, on the first day of spring,
Kula's old Tūtū Kāne saw a wonderful thing.
A poster invited, "Come One and Come All
to the Town Talent Show at the School Music Hall."

As fast as he could, Tūtū Kāne rushed home
past the corner fish market and the savings and loan.

"Kula!" he shouted as he ran up the street.
"It's your time to make history! Your chance to be seen!

Tonight there will be a town talent show,
so tune up your 'uke, get dressed, and let's go!"

The school music hall was packed to capacity.
Up front were the judges, the mayor, and his family.

Out in the crowd were friends, dads, and mommies,
a gaggle of teachers, and old Tūtū Kāne.

With a word from the mayor and his beautiful wife,
the talent show started and up came the lights.

The crowd cheered the dancers
and their balancing act.
They applauded the yodeler
in his ten-gallon hat.

They clapped for the whistler
and singers galore.

But when Kula had finished, they all wanted more.

"Bravo!" sang the singers as they rose to their feet.
"Play us another!" yodeled Yodeling Pete.

"Hana hou!" the crowd chanted. They cried out for more.
Their cheers grew so loud, they rattled the floor.

Bowing and smiling, Kula answered their calls
with an encore performance for the packed music hall.

He played his own song, "Jumping Flea," and did sing
about old Tūtū Kāne and his koa four string.

The mayor and the judges agreed with the crowd:
Kula's fabulous playing had made them all proud.

And old Tūtū Kāne was proudest that night,
watching brave little Kula have the time of his life.

about the author

Lance Wheeler spent his early years on the island of Maui. The youngest of three sons to Milton and Dr. Linda Wheeler, he enjoyed life with brothers Milton and Garrett doing everything from playing baseball with the neighborhood kids to bodysurfing at Big Beach in Mākena.

His early love for creative writing was developed as a teen while attending University Laboratory School at the University of Hawai'i at Mānoa, and refined at the University of Colorado at Boulder, where he studied communication and fine arts.

A musician at heart, this stage and film actor has been working in television for twenty years. When opportunity knocked in 1996, Wheeler answered and spent the next six years working in Los Angeles on television commercials, music videos, and feature films.

Currently, he resides on O'ahu with his wife, Kim, and son, Kula, where he performs on local television and in theatre productions. Wheeler is currently creating another children's book and a made-for-television show.

about the illustrator

Jon J. Murakami was born and raised in Honolulu, Hawai'i. He began drawing at the age of three with the encouragement of his parents and older sisters. Murakami earned a Bachelor of Fine Arts degree from the University of Hawai'i at Mānoa, where he created a daily comic strip for the student paper Ka Leo O Hawai'i. Currently a freelance cartoonist, Murakami is best known for his local greeting cards. He has also worked with Coates & Frey, Bank of Hawai'i, Aloha Airlines, and many other local businesses. His other children's books include The Original Poi Cat on O'ahu and Going to the Zoo in Hawai'i.